When I Were a Nipper...

When I Were a Nipper...

Andrew Davies

PORTICO

First published in the United Kingdom in 2011 by
Portico Books
10 Southcombe Street
London
W14 0RA

An imprint of Anova Books Company Ltd

ISBN 13: 978-1-907554-36-0

A CIP catalogue record for this book is available from
the British Library.

10 9 8 7 6 5 4 3 2 1

Reproduction by Rival Colour Ltd.
Printed and bound by 1010 Printing International Limited, China

This book can be ordered direct from the publisher.
Contact the marketing department, but try your bookshop first.

www.anovabooks.com

Contents

You Made Your Own Fun

When I were a nipper you had to make your own fun.
We didn't have fancy ball pits or tumble jungles
but we did have a soft play area.
We called it grass.

In them days you could play with your foot
for two hours and not get bored.

We had to use our imagination. A box or a suitcase were a boat or a steam engine, or an interplanetary spacecraft which could be locked to prevent aliens getting at you.

Some spacecraft smelt fishier than others.

14

We entertained our fellow tots, too.
Several rusks would change hands on the
outcome of Stan versus Vic over three rounds.
(We had three because nobody was
sure what came after three.)

The Klichko sisters were unbeaten for ages.

You Learned About Danger

Borough council playgrounds would make
your modern Health and Safety officer weep into
their clipboard, but they taught you about danger.
After one of your limbs got crushed in
the Witch's Hat, you never did it again.

19

Back then they didn't give you an ASBO,
they gave you a thick ear and you soon learned
not to sit next to the trouble-makers
...except for Humpty.

You learned exactly when to make
the leap onto Treacherous Neddy.

You learned which signs were worth reading.

You learned when there were enough
people in the house.

And when it came to freefall parachuting,
you learned to be spot-on from 3,000 feet.

Brought Up By Dogs

With both parents out earning,
childcare were often left to dog...
He weren't happy.

We weren't, neither. He never heated the bottle.

And he couldn't be fussed to fetch us a spoon.

When you were old enough, he
was there as a mate.
Albeit, a mate who liked sniffing
his friends' backsides and
relieving himself on street corners.

Sometimes it were other way
round, with you looking after the dog.
Me sister were mad for puppies.

She used to "wuv" them to within an inch of their lives.
If she'd ever found her way to Battersea Dogs' Home
we'd have been in trouble.

41

Having a dog gave them someone to boss about.
Like a boyfriend but smellier.

43

The dog would have to do what they were told.
Mind their manners at the dinner table.

Perform tricks till they got them right.

And always remember to laugh at the punchline.

There's some as had elephants as nannies.
You were quite safe.

Providing they didn't put you in with
the elephant baby.

Prams Were Substantial

When I were a nipper they made prams from
the subframes of Morris Minors. You wouldn't
get yummy mummies jogging along with these.
You needed the biceps of Geoff Capes to push one of them.

At Saint Joseph's orphanage they didn't have a pram,
they went round with a big basket of orphans.

And at Notre Dame they had a baguette.

At Saint Luke's – who were always overcrowded –
they had a Stop Me and Buy One.

You Learned A Trade Early

It's funny, even though kids were two years old,
you knew what they were going to do in life.
You could guess what Colin were going to be...

And Cockney Gary had 'black cab driver'
written all over him.

Lots of kids wanted jobs on TV.
Phil were going to be an actor on *EastEnders*...
When he could get out of the basket.

Chris didn't want a job on the farm.
He wanted to present wildlife programmes
on BBC and stare at nuthatches.

And wee Gordon started off on
completely the wrong foot.

David were always worrying if
he'd made the right decision...

73

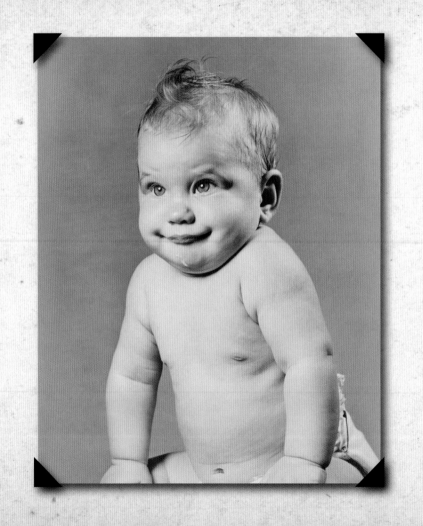

While Ed just concentrated on the big jobs.

Life Were Full Of Discoveries

When I were a nipper you had to find out about animals yourself. Could you stroke a fish?
Yes.

Did they swallow cats?
No.

Was this one entirely dead?
It were gurgling a little bit, but probably, yes.

Snakes as pets? You couldn't really
get attached to a python –
even if it got attached to you.

But tortoises were another story.
There were no stronger bond than between a boy
and his tortoise. They could double up as a goalpost
or act as an enemy sniper's helmet.

Girls weren't fussed about them.
They couldn't dress them up, nurse them or
teach them tricks.

But for a boy your own tortoise were top.

Beside The Seaside

When it came to holidays, you went to
the closest bit of sea you had.
Or river.

And if you couldn't get to either,
you made do with boating lake.

You could have a ride up on Jumbo for 6d.
Off he went with a trumpety trump - trump, trump, trump.
It were always better to sit up front.

We took a shedload of snaps with
the latest instant camera.

But sometimes it were plain miserable -
even if you did get to meet Ant and Dec.

We had loads of fun besides holidays.
The posh nippers played golf.

The clever ones read the newspaper.

The strange ones went to dance classes
and took their own partner.

And the unmusical ones tortured small dogs.

There were nothing like the healing power of ice cream.
When I were a nipper, Mr Whippy wasn't a nickname
in a House of Commons scandal, he sold lollies.
And a lolly was the perfect distraction.

It even distracted you from walking up
the right steps home.

Cakes Were A Special Event

For your birthday they'd dress you up
all smart, give you a cake, some candles
and a packet of Swan Vestas.

Or they might dress you as the Pope.

The phrase "You can't have your cake and eat it" took a bit of explanation at two years old.

In fact, you could eat it, lick it, throw it,
or use it as a high-factor suncream.

We Hated Bath Time

Bath time weren't much fun.
In fact, it were an all-round miserable experience.

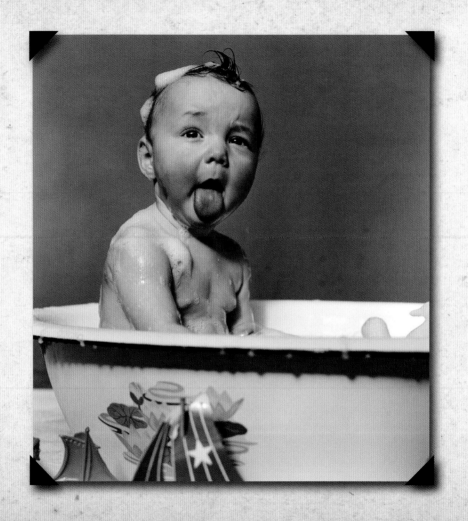

You learned pretty early on that bathwater
weren't the greatest beverage.

And sharing with a twin had its drawbacks.
Especially if he were a keen flaneller.

You also had to check out you had the same level of equipment.

It Were Never Easy...

It weren't easy being a kid. Crossing road were
difficult enough. Out front of our house were
like the First Battle of the Somme.

129

Sometimes they put a pond
slap bang in your way.

And postboxes were annoying, too.
Dad said Santa wouldn't come till I were
tall enough to post me own letter.

If you started dealing penny chews
in playground, police came down
on you like a ton of bricks.

It were always better to pay them off.
Thousand-piece jigsaw were the standard backhander.

When I were a nipper you didn't mind that Teddy were always snooping on what you were up to.

Or that the bloke who ran the Doll's Hospital was quite obviously a serial killer.

141

But oh, the grief of missing Andy Pandy and Looby Loo.
Knowing you'd failed to wave Andy and Teddy
"Goodbye" was sometimes too much to bear...

Picture Credit Where
Picture Credit's Due

Other books in the series:

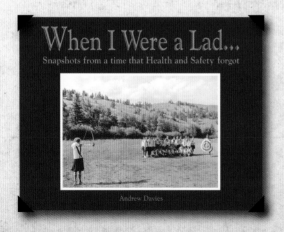

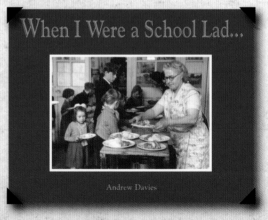